SNOOPY AND CHARLIE BROWN

THE PEANUTS MOVIE

by SCHULZ

STORYBOOK

Peanuts created by
CHARLES M. SCHULZ

PUFFIN

PUFFIN BOOKS

UK | USA | Canada | Ireland | Australia
India | New Zealand | South Africa

Puffin Books is part of the Penguin Random House group of companies
whose addresses can be found at global.penguinrandomhouse.com.

puffinbooks.com

First published 2015
001

Printed in Italy

A CIP catalogue record for this book is available from the British Library

ISBN: 978–0–141–36688–3

It's a wintry school morning and Charlie Brown is still tucked up in bed. As he lies there, he can hear his little sister, Sally, on the phone.

"No school today?" she says. "A snow day? Hooray – it's a snow day!"

Charlie Brown rushes to get dressed.
By the time he gets outside, his friends are
already there. They're all busy skating and
playing ice hockey.

Everyone loves a snow day!

Charlie Brown is carrying his new kite. "This could be the day," he says to himself. "The day I finally fly my kite." He holds the string firmly and runs as fast as he can.

"It's FLYING!" he shouts.

But, as he runs, the string gets caught round his ankles. The kite lifts him up into the air and spins him about, until he ends up hanging upside down in the Kite-Eating Tree!

Charlie Brown untangles himself and pulls down the tattered remains of his kite.

"It's going to be a long winter," he sighs.

"What kind of person tries to fly a kite in the middle of winter?" Lucy shouts. "You will never get that kite to fly."

Everyone turns to look at Charlie Brown and begins to laugh.

Suddenly, the sound of a moving truck's horn sends the gang running to the wooden fence.

"Hey, there's a new kid moving in!"

The next morning, as the Peanuts gang sit in class, the door opens and the teacher enters followed by someone else.

It's the new kid. And it's a girl. A girl with beautiful red hair!

Charlie Brown's heart starts to beat faster!
He really wants to become her friend.

As the Little Red-Haired Girl takes her seat, the teacher hands out test papers.

How is Charlie Brown ever going to be able to concentrate now?

Once the test is finished, the Little Red-Haired Girl gets up to hand in her paper. As she walks away, her pink pencil falls to the floor . . . rolls . . . and stops in front of Charlie Brown.

"She nibbles her pencil just like I do!" he says, examining it.

Charlie Brown doesn't know what to do! His heart is pounding and his knees are weak. But he will never be brave enough to speak to her.

He decides to visit Lucy. "I need your advice," he says. "There's a girl I'd like to impress."

"Girls don't like failures, Charlie Brown! If you really want to impress a girl," she says, "you need to show her you're a winner!"

Lucy hands him a book. It's called *10 Ways to Become a Winner*.

Charlie Brown takes the book home, but as he begins to read he hears a strange noise. He decides to go and investigate.

It's Snoopy and Sally, and she's holding a cowboy hat.

"What are you doing?" he asks.

"I'm going to be a rodeo star in the school talent show!" she cries. "Yee-haw!"

This gives Charlie Brown a brilliant idea!

He will win the talent show!

And then the Little Red-Haired Girl will be bound to notice him.

Charlie Brown pulls out his magic set and begins to practise!

Snoopy decides no magic act is complete without a loyal assistant and rushes to get his best bow tie.

On the night of the talent show, Charlie Brown waits nervously in the wings. Nothing can go wrong now!

He watches Sally onstage. "Ride 'em, cowgirl!" she shouts.

But something is wrong.

The audience begins laughing at Sally as she tries to lasso a cardboard cow. She looks nervously at Charlie Brown.

Charlie Brown decides he must help her!

So, rather than perform his magic act, he leaps on to the stage and pretends to be a cow. He knows he looks ridiculous but he must help his little sister.

"Rope me!" he calls to her. "Moo!"

Sally's eyes light up and she swings the lasso over her head. She throws the rope round Charlie Brown and pulls tight. The crowd goes wild!

Charlie Brown is so embarrassed, and to make things worse he spots the Little Red-Haired Girl in the crowd.

After the failure of the talent show, Charlie Brown concentrates harder than ever on *10 Ways to Become a Winner*. He doesn't even hear the phone ring.

"Your girlfriend's on the phone," Sally calls out, teasing him.

"It can't be," he thinks. "The Little Red-Haired Girl is phoning me?"

But it's only Peppermint Patty.
She tells Charlie Brown that she has
signed him up to make cupcakes
for the Winter Dance.

Charlie Brown sighs.
Why would *he* want
to go to the Winter
Dance?

That night, as Charlie Brown takes out the recycling, through the window opposite he can just make out the figure of a girl with a cloud of whirling red hair dancing around.

"She likes to dance!" he says.

CRASH! BANG! BUMP!

Following a strange sound, Sally and Snoopy carefully push open the door to Charlie Brown's room, and there they find him dancing with a huge smile on his face.

"I'm going to dance with her!" Charlie Brown cries, twirling around.

But Charlie Brown needs help, and Snoopy is just the beagle to do it. He goes straight to his doghouse and pulls out the dancing kit.

He lays some footprints on the floor in a simple pattern, and then encourages Charlie Brown to try the steps.

"One, two, three, four. One, two, three, four," whispers Charlie Brown under his breath, as he moves around the room.

After many hours of practising, Charlie Brown begins to get the hang of it.

The Winter Dance is tonight and the school gym has been transformed!

The girls' dance competition begins. Charlie Brown watches as the Little Red-Haired Girl takes her turn and her friends begin cheering and whooping.

"Well, I think we know who our winner is!"
Franklin calls.

"And now it's the gentlemen's turn!"
he continues.

Charlie Brown's heart beats fast as he takes his
place on the dance floor.

With a deep breath, he begins performing the
dance just as Snoopy taught him!

But suddenly his shoe flies off and hits the fire sprinkler on the ceiling, sending cold water spraying down on to the party.

"This is not how it was supposed to end," he says.

Just then, the Little Red-Haired Girl walks over to Charlie Brown and begins to tell him how much she admires him. "You showed compassion for your sister at the talent show, and here at the dance you were brave and funny."

The Little Red-Haired Girl wants to be his friend because he never gave up. Charlie Brown can't stop smiling!

It feels really good to be Charlie Brown.